Clock Poems

Compiled by John Foster

Contents

Acknowledgements

The Editor and Publisher wish to thank the following who have kindly given permission for the use of copyright material:

John Foster for 'Home time' and 'The old clock' both © 1991 John Foster; Gwenda Izzet for 'Tick Tock' © 1991 Gwenda Izzet; Judith Nicholls for 'Time for . . .?' © 1991 Judith Nicholls.

Tick Tock

Tick tock—eight o'clock.
Out of bed, sleepy head.

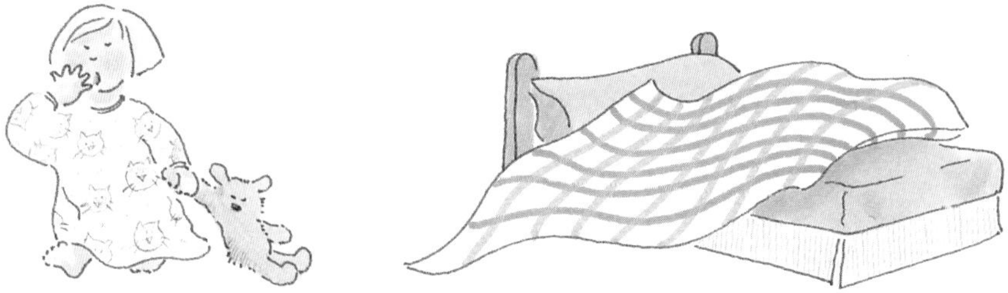

Tick tock—nine o'clock.
School begins, get out your things.

Tick tock—twelve o'clock.
It's time to eat, what a treat.

Tick tock—three o'clock.
It's time for fun, we skip and run.

Tick tock—five o'clock.
It's time for tea for you and me.

Tick tock—eight o'clock.
Back to bed, sleepy head.

Gwenda Izzet

Time for . . .?

Christopher Sweet tucked his feet
down to the bottom
of the warm, warm sheet.
How many times
did the Church clock strike?
One, two, three, four, five,
six, seven, EIGHT!

Caroline Tate is always late,
she's only just running
through the old school gate!
How many times
did the school bell chime?
One, two, three, four, five,
six, seven, eight, NINE!

Oliver Lee can't wait for tea,
school's nearly finished for him and me!
How many rings till we're all free?
One, two, THREE!

Nicola Head won't go to bed.
'Chase her up the stairs then'
her mother said.
How many times
did the clock strike then?
One, two, three, four, five,
six, seven, eight, nine, TEN!

Marilyn Heap is fast asleep;
listen at the door
but you won't hear a peep!
How many times
did the Church clock strike?
One, two, three, four, five,
six, seven, eight, nine, ten,
eleven, twelve . . . MIDNIGHT!

Judith Nicholls

The old clock

The old clock
Has stopped.
What can we do?

What's the time?
Half-past two.

The old clock
Has stopped.
It won't go any more.

What's the time?
Half-past four.

The old clock
Has stopped.
It's playing tricks.

What's the time?
Half-past six.

The old clock
Has stopped.
Hurry up! You're late.

What's the time?
Half-past eight.

The old clock
Has stopped.
It won't start again.

What's the time?
Half-past ten.

The old clock
Has stopped.
What shall we do?

Go out and buy
A clock that's new!

John Foster

Home time

The clock strikes three.
The clock strikes three.
Down by the school gate
Mum's waiting for me.

The clock strikes three.
The clock strikes three.
It's time to go home
To watch the TV!

John Foster